Then he saved their lives, and they swore never to leave him.

We give you the Secret-Hairy-Snot-Tooth Oath of Devotion.

When he moved house, Billy found ANOTHER monster.

Hello. My name's Sparkle-Bogey.

One thing was certain – Billy's life would never be the same **AGAIN**...

Contents

BILLY

AND THE MINI MONSTERS

MONSTERS AT CHRISTMAS

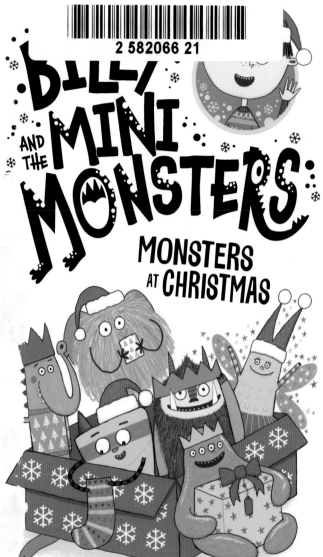

Illustrated by
ZANNA DAVIDSON · MELANIE WILLIAMSON

Meet Billy...

Billy was just an ordinary boy living an ordinary life, until **ONE NIGHT** he found five **MINI MONSTERS** in his sock drawer.

Gloop

Peep

Fang-Face

Captain Snott

Trumpet

Chapter 1
Letters to Father Christmas

Billy and Ruby were sitting in Billy's bedroom with the Mini Monsters, feeling VERY excited. It was nearly Christmas!

"I hope it snows," said Billy. "I've asked Mum and Dad for a sledge for Christmas."

Snow would make it my best Christmas ever.

"What happens at Christmas?" asked Peep. "We've never had a proper Christmas before."

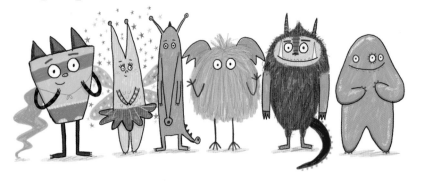

"Father Christmas brings us presents on Christmas Eve," explained Ruby.

"But he doesn't come to *naughty children*," added Billy.

He only brings presents if you've been GOOD.

"And now," Billy said to the Mini Monsters, "I need to have a **Top Secret** chat with Ruby."

"Actually," said Fang-Face, "WE need to have a **Top Secret** chat, too. We're going to our drawer..."

Billy waited until the monsters had gone. "I've been feeling a bit worried," he whispered to Ruby. "If Father Christmas doesn't **know** about the Mini Monsters, he might not bring them presents!"

So I've written him a letter...

8

Dear Father Christmas,

Please could you bring presents for my Mini Monsters?
You might think they've been naughty, but they've
tried REALLY hard to be good. I will leave out
stockings for them. Here are things they might like:

- A new eyeball for Gloop
(He's lost one.)

- A Christmassy cape for Captain
Snott (He really loves capes.)

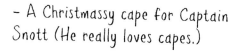

- Vegan cheese for Trumpet
(It's his favourite food.)

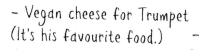

- A spider-catcher for Fang-Face
(He's a bit scared of spiders
after our camping trip.)

- A coat for Peep (He gets cold easily.)

- Eco-glitter for Sparkle-Bogey
(She eats it. A lot.)

From Billy

"Ooh!" said Ruby. "I've done my letter to Father Christmas, too."

Dear Father Christmas,

For Christmas, please can I have:

- a unicorn

- a magic wand

- a Tyrannosaurus rex

- a water pistol

- lots of chocolate!!

Love Ruby XXX

"Maybe I should ask for something for Sparkle-Bogey, as she's my monster," said Ruby. "Do you think I can ask Father Christmas to bring her bogeys?"

"I'm not sure," Billy replied.

"I'll add it, just in case," said Ruby.

ps And bogeys (If that's allowed.)

Then Billy and Ruby put their letters in an envelope.

Billy wrote the address.

Father Christmas,
   Top Secret Christmas Workshop,
   North Pole.

"I'll give it to Mum to post," said Billy. "It's only two weeks till Christmas. I hope Father Christmas gets our letters in time."

Just then, their dad called from downstairs. "Billy! Ruby! Time to decorate the tree!"

"**Hooray!**" said Billy. "Now it's really starting to feel like Christmas!"

Meanwhile, in the sock drawer...

What is the secret thing we need to discuss?

We don't know what Father Christmas **LOOKS** like!

Billy said he has a red suit and a white beard. But that's all we know!

Don't worry. I know **EXACTLY** what Father Christmas looks like.

He has three horns and a long cape.

15

What's the matter, Peep?

Ruby said Father Christmas only comes if you've been **GOOD**.

What happens if he doesn't visit Billy because we're always getting him into trouble?

Oh no! What shall we do?

Let's make Billy a present ourselves, in case Father Christmas doesn't come.

Chapter 2
The Christmas Tree

"Look," said Billy's dad, proudly. "This year, we've got our biggest tree EVER!"

Wow! It's HUGE!

Billy's mum opened up a chest, full of decorations. "Be careful with them," she said. "These decorations are very delicate. They belonged to my mum, and some of them belonged to *her* mum."

This was my mum's favourite.

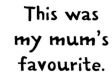

Billy and his family hung the tinsel, and the lights, and the baubles until...

...at last, the tree was done.

"What about the *fairy*?" asked Ruby. "I'll need a ladder to reach the top of the tree," said Dad. "But first, it's time to visit our neighbours for some mince pies!"

Billy's mum was still gazing at the tree. "Isn't it *magical!*" she said. "Do you believe in magic?" asked Ruby.

"I do when I see the fairy on the tree," her mum replied. "That's what makes Christmas magical for me."

"We'll do the fairy as soon as we get back," said Dad. "Don't forget to close the door, Billy," he added. "We don't want the dog getting up to mischief!"

Billy closed the door, then
hurried upstairs to his room.
"We're going out,"
he told the Mini Monsters.
"While we're gone,
whatever you do,
DON'T touch
the tree downstairs."

It's covered in
lots of decorations.
They're **REALLY**
precious.

"Of course we won't touch the tree, Billy," said the Mini Monsters.

Billy grabbed his coat and waved goodbye to the Mini Monsters. "See you when I'm back! I'll bring you some mince pies..."

As soon as Billy had gone...

I can't wait to see the tree!

Ooh! It's so pretty!

Let's swing on tinsel!

Chime the bells!

WAIT! Billy said we mustn't touch the tree.

But we could HELP! Look, they forgot to put up the fairy.

27

28

Chapter 3
Dog vs Tree

Just then, the door BURST open and the dog bounded into the room.

"Aaargh!"

cried Trumpet.

"Don't worry! I'll
scare him off," said
Fang-Face. He raised
his arms and rushed
at the dog.

Trumpet, Gloop
and Captain
Snott all ran
towards the tree.

31

Fang-Face growled at the dog.
The dog growled back.

By now, Trumpet, Gloop and
Captain Snott had started to
climb the tree.

Fang-Face growled
EVEN louder.

The dog came
EVEN closer.

"I'm not sure your plan is working," Sparkle-Bogey called down to Fang-Face.

"The dog really doesn't seem very scared of you," added Peep.

"No, he doesn't," agreed Fang-Face.

Help!

"Now would be a good time for you to do one of your cheese-powered parps, Trumpet," said Fang-Face.

"I'll try," said Trumpet.

But nothing happened.

"I've been trying to give up eating cheese," said Trumpet. "Ever since I found out it was bad for the planet!"

The Mini Monsters looked down. The dog was now VERY close to Fang-Face.

"Fang-Face is going to be EATEN!" cried Gloop. "We have to DO something."

"Quick!" said Captain Snott. "Let's form a line."

At the last moment...

Hurry! Take my hand!

...Captain Snott grabbed Fang-Face and swung him to safety.

"Phew!" said Fang-Face. "That hound can't get me now."

"Er..." said Gloop. "I'm not so sure about that..."

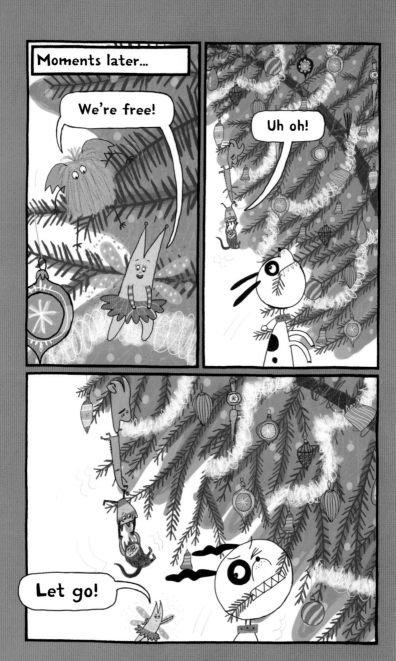

THUD!

Oh dear!

Chapter 4
A Christmas Disaster

"That was lovely!" said Billy's dad, as they reached the front door.

I do love a mince pie.

"And now we've got the ladder from the garage," said his mum, "we can put the fairy on the tree."

"That's strange," thought Billy as they walked in. "I'm sure I shut the sitting room door."

When they went into the sitting room, a **TERRIBLE SIGHT** met their eyes...

"It must have been the dog," said Billy's dad. "But I thought I asked you to shut the door, Billy?"

"I'm sure I did," said Billy.

"Never mind," said Billy's mum. "It doesn't matter. Let's get this tree up again."

But Billy could see she looked **really** sad.

So many baubles are broken, Mum.

And your fairy is broken too.

"They're just *things*, aren't they," said Billy's mum, giving them a wobbly smile. "And we mustn't let it ruin Christmas."

Billy and Ruby helped put the tree back up.

They swept up the broken baubles...

...and re-hung
the tinsel.

The tree
looked a bit
sorry for itself.

Then Billy's parents left, with
the dog. "I feel terrible," said Billy.
"I must have left the door open."

And now
Mum is
really sad!

But then, from behind the log
basket... came the Mini Monsters.
They looked miserable, too.

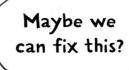

Maybe we can fix this?

"I don't know if there's anything we can do to make it better," said Billy.

Mum's decorations are smashed.

I know what we can do!

"We can make NEW decorations for the tree," said Ruby.

"And we'll help too!" said the Mini Monsters.

"It's a plan," said Billy.

Over the next two weeks, the Mini Monsters were hard at work...

Uh oh!

Chapter 5
The Unusual Fairy

By Christmas Eve, Billy, Ruby and the Mini Monsters had finished the last of the decorations for the tree.

"Mum and Dad are busy in the kitchen," whispered Billy. "Let's put up the decorations so it's a surprise."

They all crept into the sitting room. The tree looked very bare.

"What have you made, Mini Monsters?" Ruby asked.

The Mini Monsters proudly held out their decorations.

When they'd hung all the decorations, Sparkle-Bogey sprinkled glitter over the branches.

"Now if you all hide," Billy told the Mini Monsters, "Ruby and I will go and get Mum and Dad."

Oh no! Look at the top of the tree!

"We forgot to make a new fairy!" said Peep.

"And the fairy was Billy's mum's favourite thing!" added Gloop.

"What are we going to do?" said Trumpet. "There has to be a *fairy*."

Don't worry, I'LL be the fairy!

"What if you get

FOUND OUT?"

said Captain Snott.

But by then it was *too late*.

The sitting room door started to open. The other Mini Monsters dashed behind the log basket, just in time...

"Oh!" said Billy's mum. "The tree looks amazing!"

Thank you!

Then she noticed Sparkle-Bogey at the top of the tree. "You even made a... *fairy*? It looks **so real**."

"It's almost as if it's... **alive**," said Dad.

Billy had to do something to distract his parents, and fast.

COUGH!

COUGH!

COUGH!

"I think he just swallowed some glitter," said Ruby.

"You two must be getting tired," said Mum. "Let's hang up the stockings and then it's time for bed."

But once Billy was in his pyjamas, he crept down the stairs again. He had six little stockings.

One for each of the Mini Monsters!

Back upstairs, Billy tucked the Mini Monsters into their sock sleeping bags, in the sock drawer.

Good night! See you on Christmas morning!

"Good night," said Billy. And very soon, he was fast asleep.

One by one, the Mini Monsters fell asleep too. All except Peep.

"I'm going to stay up to see Father Christmas!" Peep decided.

What's that in the sky?

Monsters, wake up!

While Billy slept...

Quick! Let's go downstairs.

There's Father Christmas!

64

Chapter 6
Christmas Magic

As soon as Billy woke on Christmas morning, he scooped up the Mini Monsters and called for Ruby.

"Let's go downstairs and see if Father Christmas came."

We've all got stockings!

Together, they opened their
stockings.

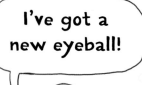

I've got a
new eyeball!

Mmm. Vegan
cheese!

Captain Snott put
on his new cape.

Just for today,
I'm Captain
Christmas!

"I'll never be scared of spiders again," said Fang-Face.

"Father Christmas brought me everything I wanted, too," said Ruby. "Billy, what did you get?"

"I've got a tangerine," said Billy. "And some chocolate coins... and **what are these**? I didn't ask for anything else."

"They're from us," said Peep. "We made them. Each book is about our adventures with you."

"**Thank you!**" gasped Billy.

Then Billy felt something, right at the bottom of his stocking.

"Oh! It's a note. From Father Christmas!"

"What does it say?" asked Ruby.

Look outside your window and see your Christmas wish come true.

From Father Christmas

Billy and Ruby rushed to the window and pulled back the curtains.

"**Wow!**" said Billy. "**It's snowing!**"

After breakfast, Billy and Ruby
went outside to play with their
friends from next door.
The Mini Monsters were
very excited to see the snow.

When you're ready, come in for hot chocolate.

Billy and Ruby said goodbye to their friends and hurried inside.

"Where's Sparkle-Bogey?"
said Billy.

"She stayed inside," said Captain
Snott. "She said she had something
important to do."

Just as Billy and Ruby sat down
for their hot chocolates, their
mum came into the kitchen.

"The strangest thing just happened," she said. "I was looking at the fairy on the tree, and she **winked** at me, then sprinkled me with glitter!"

This is definitely my most magical Christmas ever!

All about the MINI MONSTERS

CAPTAIN SNOTT →

LIKES EATING: bogeys.

SPECIAL SKILL:
can glow in the dark.

SCARE
FACTOR:
5/10

← GLOOP

LIKES EATING: cake.

SPECIAL SKILL:
very stre-e-e-e-tchy.
Gloop can also swallow his own
eyeballs and make them reappear
on any part of his body.

SCARE
FACTOR:
4/10

FANG-FACE →

LIKES EATING:
socks, school ties, paper, or
anything that comes his way.

SPECIAL SKILL:
has massive fangs.

SCARE
FACTOR:
9/10

TRUMPET →

LIKES EATING:
vegan cheese.

SPECIAL SKILL:
amazingly powerful
cheese-powered parps.

SCARE FACTOR:
7/10

(taking into
account his parps)

PEEP

LIKES EATING: very small flies.

SPECIAL SKILL: can fly (but
not very far, or very well).

SCARE FACTOR:
0/10 (unless you're afraid of
small hairy things)

SPARKLE-BOGEY →

LIKES EATING:
eco-glitter and bogeys.

SPECIAL SKILL:
can shoot out clouds
of glitter.

SCARE FACTOR:
5/10 (if you're scared of
pink sparkly glitter)

Series editor: Becky Walker
Designed by Brenda Cole
Cover design by Hannah Cobley

First published in 2021 by Usborne Publishing Ltd., Usborne House,
83-85 Saffron Hill, London EC1N 8RT, England. usborne.com
Copyright © 2021 Usborne Publishing Ltd. UKE